For Sheila, with love
J.B.

For Joe
x
R.B.

First published in 2013 by Scholastic Children's Books
Euston House, 24 Eversholt Street, London NW1 1DB
a division of Scholastic Ltd
www.scholastic.com
London ~ New York ~ Toronto ~ Sydney ~ Auckland ~ Mexico City ~ New Delhi ~ Hong Kong

PB ISBN 978 1 407132 36 5

The Best Present

Written by
Janet Bingham

Illustrated by
Rosalind Beardshaw

SCHOLASTIC

Little Brown Bear and Daddy were going on a visit.

"Hurry up, Daddy!" called Little Brown Bear, racing ahead.
"You're walking too slowly. I can't wait to see Grandma!"

It was a long walk to Grandma's house. On the way
they passed a mouse carrying a beautiful, shiny nut.
"Perhaps it's a present for somebody," said Daddy.

That gave Little
Brown Bear an idea.
"Let's find a present
for Grandma!" he said.

So Little Brown Bear began to look for a present.
He found some bright red and yellow autumn leaves.
But they were muddy.

"These are no good," said Little Brown Bear.
"I'll find a better present for Grandma.

I'll find the
**best present
of all!**"

So Little Brown Bear kept looking for a present.
Daddy picked up a flower.
   "Shall we give this to Grandma?" he asked.

"Yes!" laughed Little Brown Bear.
"It's pretty and it smells nice.
This is the best present of all!"

After a while Daddy said, "Let's stop for a drink."
They scooped up some icy-cold water.

"Be careful," warned Daddy. But the flower slipped from
Little Brown Bear's grasp, and the stream carried it away.

"Whoops!" cried Little Brown Bear.

"Never mind," said Daddy. "Perhaps somebody
else will find it. They will think the stream
has brought them a gift."

So Little Brown Bear kept on looking for a present. Next he found a fluffy blue feather.

Daddy stroked the feather over Little Brown Bear's nose and made him laugh.

"It's tickly," Little Brown Bear giggled.
"Grandma will love it.
This is the best present of all!"

Little Brown Bear held the feather up as
he walked, and it shivered in the breeze.
Suddenly, a gust of wind whipped it away.
He tried to catch it, but it flew high
into the air!

"What a shame," said Daddy.
"But I'm sure you will find an
even better present for Grandma."
And just then, it started to snow…

Little Brown Bear and Daddy watched the soft white flakes float down from the sky. "Every snowflake is different," said Daddy. "That's what Grandma told me when I was a little bear."

Little Brown Bear caught
a snowflake and looked
at it carefully. He had
never seen anything
so magical.

"Grandma will love it,"
he said to himself.
This is the very
best present of all!"

At last, Little Brown Bear and Daddy
reached Grandma's house. She came
out to meet them with a big smile.

"I found you a flower, Grandma,"
said Little Brown Bear, "but it floated
away in the stream. And I found you
a feather, but it flew away…"
He took a deep breath.

"But now I've brought you
the best present of all.
It's a snowflake!"

Little Brown Bear opened his paw carefully.
"Oh!" he gasped. "Where is it?"
All that was left was a tiny drop of water.

"It has melted away," said Grandma gently.
"Your paw is too warm to hold a snowflake."

Little Brown Bear felt sad. "I wanted to bring you the best present of all!" he said.

Grandma cuddled him close and smiled. "You are a kind little bear," she said. "But you don't need to bring me a present…

"...because YOU are the best present of all!"